Text copyright © 2024 by Janie Havemeyer | Illustrations copyright © 2024 by Jean Claverie
Edited by Amy Novesky and Kate Riggs; designed by Rita Marshall
Published in 2024 by Creative Editions P. O. Box 227, Mankato, MN 56002 USA
Creative Editions is an imprint of The Creative Company www.thecreativecompany.us
Library of Congress Cataloging-in-Publication Data
Names: Havemeyer, Janie, author. | Claverie, Jean, 1946– illustrator.
Title: Motorcycle queen : the life of Bessie Stringfield / by Janie Havemeyer ; illustrated by Jean Claverie.
Description: First edition. | Mankato, Minnesota : Creative Editions, 2024. | Audience: Ages 8– 12 years | Audience: Grades 4–6 |
Summary: "An illustrated picture book about Bessie Stringfield, who shocked 1930s society as a woman who not only rode a
motorcycle but also performed stunts and traveled solo cross-country, earning the nickname "Motorcycle Queen.""—Provided by publisher.
Identifiers: LCCN 2023045890 (print) | LCCN 2023045891 (ebook) | ISBN 9781568463568 (hardcover) | ISBN 9781640004115 (ebook)
Subjects: LCSH: Stringfield, Bessie, 1911– 1993—Juvenile literature. | Women motorcyclists—United States—Biography—Juvenile literature. |
Motorcyclists—United States—Biography—Juvenile literature. | Discrimination in sports—United States—Juvenile literature. | American
Motorcyclist Association—History—Juvenile literature. | African American women—Biography—Juvenile literature. | African Americans—
Biography—Juvenile literature. Classification: LCC GV1060.2.S75 H38 2024 (print) | LCC GV1060.2.S75 (ebook) |
DDC 796.7/5092 [B]—dc23/eng/20231030   LC record available at https://lccn.loc.gov/2023045890
LC ebook record available at https://lccn.loc.gov/202304589   First edition 9 8 7 6 5 4 3 2 1

MOTORCYCLE QUEEN

The Life of Bessie Stringfield

Janie Havemeyer illustrated by Jean Claverie

CREATIVE EDITIONS

If Bessie didn't ride, she didn't want to live.

On her Scout motorcycle, Bessie roared down
the road, gripping the handlebars. She banked
around corners, crouching low over her bike.
She felt the cool wind on her face. She felt fierce.
On her motorcycle, Bessie felt free.

Bessie waved to her neighbors as she sped by.
A few waved back, but most shook their heads.
A girl on a motorcycle—it just wasn't ladylike.

Bessie Stringfield was sixteen when she rode her first motorcycle. She said it was a birthday gift from her mother, but Bessie told tall tales. She made up stories about her childhood. The truth was hard.

Whenever she could, Bessie snuck off to ride. She knew Black girls were asking for trouble if they made too much noise. So, Bessie rode down narrow dirt roads, where no one would hear her.

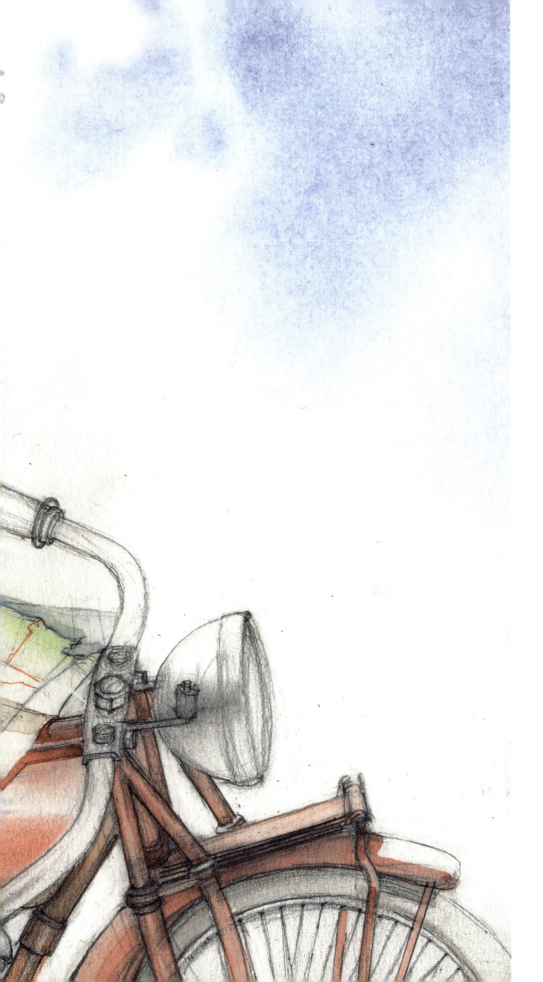

One day, Bessie packed a saddlebag with clothes and food. She would follow her dream and ride on the open road. The Lord would help her decide where to go. She flipped a penny onto her road map. The coin landed in Georgia. Bessie knew staying in the South might mean trouble, but God had spoken.

Bessie slipped into her leather jacket and tall black boots. She tied the straps of her cap tightly under her chin. "Precious Lord, take my hand, lead me on, let me stand," she sang the words of her favorite hymn. Then she straddled her bike and turned the key. Scout gave a deep, low rumble. Bessie sped off, louder than a firecracker.

On her motorcycle, Bessie felt free.

9

Bessie roared over hills, glided down roads curved like the moon, splashed across shallow streams. At night she slept deep in the woods, hidden from sight. At night the crickets chirped. In the morning the crows cackled.

The day a pickup truck sped up behind her, honking loudly, Bessie put her head down, twisting the throttle harder. The truck kept on honking, pulling closer, then BUMP! Scout rumbled off the road like a wounded bull. Bessie's hands scraped gravel as they fell. CRASH! The truck sped by, still blasting its horn. **HONK!**

Bessie lay next to Scout, her body twisted and bruised. Slowly, she eased herself up into a sitting position, the dust settling about them. Scout had a few scratches, too. Bessie untied the scarf around her neck and spit-polished them up.

That's when she saw a sign.

A crowd lined an oval track where motorcycle riders kicked up clouds of dust. Bessie rolled her bike up to the starting line for the next race. She wore a handkerchief over her face to keep the dirt out of her mouth. No one noticed her. When a man lowered a green flag, she and the riders zoomed off.

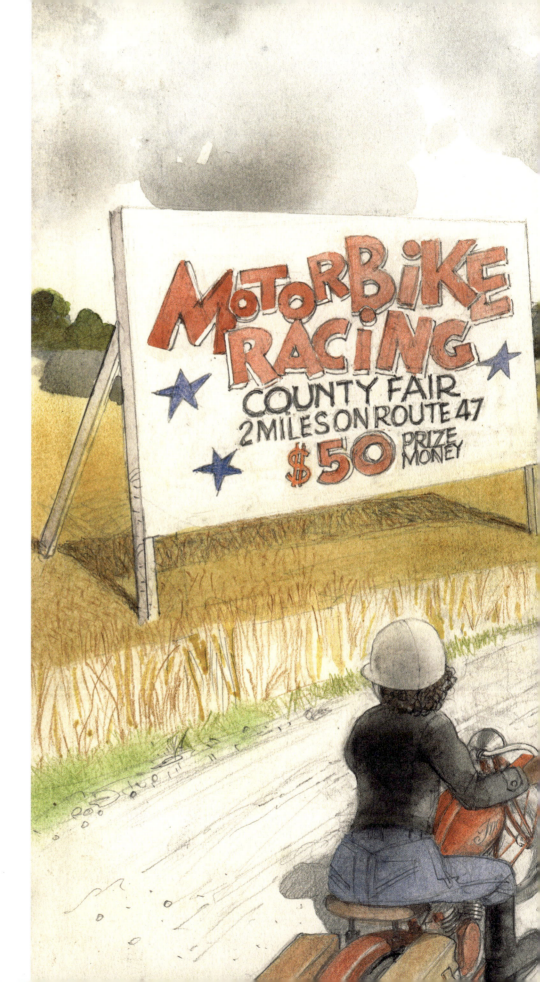

Bessie banked hard around curves. She sped down a hill and back up another. One motorcycle flipped over, sending its rider flying. Now she was neck and neck with only two others. She twisted Scout's throttle as hard as it would go. She crossed the finish line first by five seconds.

On her motorcycle, Bessie felt fierce.

When all the riders gathered, Bessie pushed the kickstand down and stepped off Scout. She took off her handkerchief and cap, and the bikers went quiet.

Bessie looked around at the crowd. She knew what they were thinking. Nice girls don't ride bikes. And she was a Black girl, to boot. Bessie jumped back on Scout and flew off faster than a hot knife through butter.

At an Esso gas station, the attendant gave her food, water, and free gas for being so brave. But he warned her, "It's not safe for a girl by y'all self out here." Bessie nodded. She already knew that. But she thanked him for his kindness.

Bessie headed north. The wind was cold on her face. Her fingers felt numb. Her neck burned. She didn't feel fierce. She didn't feel free.

In Ohio, Bessie thought she'd be safer, until she heard a siren behind her. She pulled over. A tall policeman got out of his cruiser.

WEEEE

He said girls didn't belong on bikes. Bessie smiled and asked, "Sir, will you let me prove you wrong?" The officer tailed her for a mile on the road. Then he tapped his horn and sped off. Bessie whispered a prayer of thanks.

For the next few weeks, Bessie stuck to the back roads. She slept under trees, hidden by the leaves. She drank from streams. She ate apples, plums, and berries that grew in the wild. Sometimes Bessie met Black folks who offered her a meal and a warm place to sleep. They couldn't believe she rode a motorcycle.

Bessie had been on the road for two months. She was tired of moving, hiding, looking over her shoulder. When she heard the buzzing of motorbikes at a carnival, she stopped. "Step right up!" yelled a loud man in a long black coat. "Watch death-defying demons on the Wall of Death!" Bessie bought a ticket for a quarter. She climbed up a staircase to a wooden viewing platform. Inside a bowl-shaped tank, four motorcycles sped up and down the slanted walls, just missing one another, sometimes only by inches. The audience hooted and cheered.

I could do that, she thought. But first she needed to learn a few new tricks.

On a dirt road west of town, Bessie practiced sliding off her bike and leaping back on. She raced up steep hills, made hairpin turns, and sped back down.

That night, she slept in the woods. Lying on her bike with her head resting on the handlebars, she watched shooting stars streak across the sky.

The next morning, just as the carnival was getting started, Bessie dusted Scout's saddle. She polished Scout's cylinders until they shone. She swung her leg over the leather seat and turned the key. Scout growled to life.

At the carnival gate, Bessie leaped onto the saddle, planting her boots firmly beneath her. When she revved the engine, Scout glided forward. Slowly and carefully, Bessie stood up tall. All five feet, two inches of her. She raised her left foot and planted it firmly on the handlebars. She twisted the throttle with her boot. Scout picked up speed. Bessie stretched her hands out to her sides. She looked like a figurehead poised on the prow of a ship.

By the time she'd reached the man in the black coat, a crowd was following her. Bessie took off her cap and goggles. The crowd cheered. No one had ever seen a girl perform tricks on a motorcycle.

The next day Bessie was a solo act.

The Motorcycle Queen raced up the slanted side of the Wall of Death. When she got to the top where it was steepest, she made a sharp left turn. She raced sideways along the top of the bowl, defying gravity. She was flying.

On her motorcycle, Bessie was free.

But Bessie wanted to do more than just stunts on her bike. She knew her life was meant for a higher purpose.

In 1941, America began fighting a war in Europe. The army needed motorcycle riders, but they weren't interested in girls. Bessie tried out anyway. She passed every test. An army captain gave her a uniform and a new blue Harley-Davidson bike with a military crest. Bessie was now the first female dispatch rider enlisted to deliver secret messages between U.S. army bases.

Soon Bessie was racing over hills and plowing through forests from one army base to another. She rode through pelting rain and the dry heat of deserts. Harley growled and smoked beneath her. When she couldn't cross a river, she made her own bridge using rope and tree limbs. She delivered one message after another, rarely stopping to rest, always zooming off on the next assignment. The top-secret documents tucked into her pouch might help the U.S. win the war.

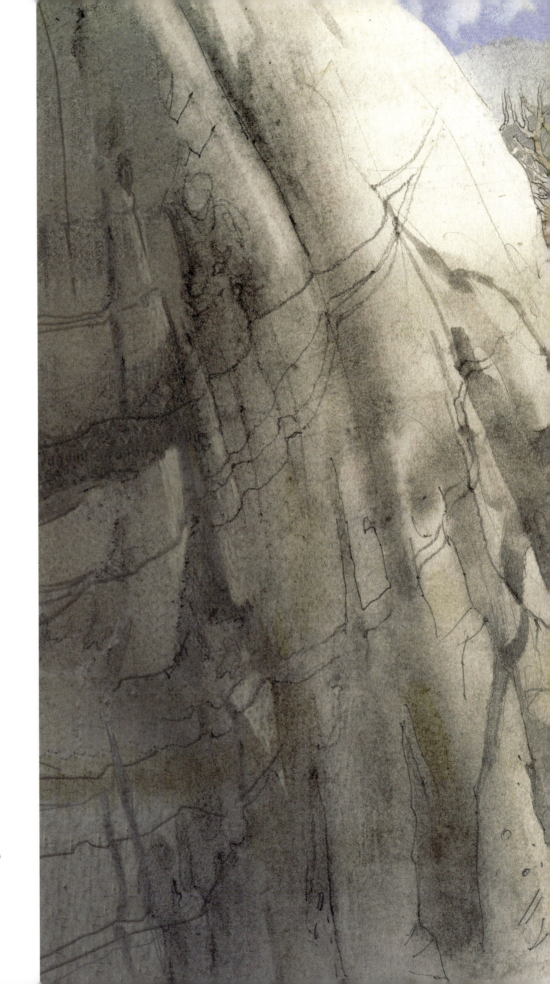

When the war ended, Bessie didn't stop moving. She explored more of the world on a motorbike.

When she grew tired of wandering, she bought a house in Florida. She rode around Miami and to church every Sunday. Reporters took notice and began to write about her. They called her the Motorcycle Queen of Miami.

In the annual parade, Bessie led a pack of motorcycle riders. She was the only woman, but she was used to that. Her two poodles Sabu and Rodney sat on her knees. Bessie waved to the cheering crowd. She sat up tall on her Harley. She revved her engine. The crowd clapped and hooted back.

Bessie was loud. She was fierce and free. She was Bessie.

Author's Note

This story is based on the life of Bessie Stringfield. Bessie was a storyteller, and some of the things she shared, especially about her childhood, have since been proven false. It is likely that Bessie made up facts about her parents and where she grew up because the truth was hard. Bessie was born in 1911, in North Carolina, and life there wasn't easy. Jim Crow laws told Black people what they could or couldn't do. If you broke a rule, you could end up dead. A good guess is that Bessie's family may not have thought it was safe for her to be riding a motorbike. Later in life, Bessie said she had been adopted by a wealthy family who gave her a motorbike for her 16th birthday. She never mentioned her real family in North Carolina.

What we do know for sure is that from 1930 to 1940, Bessie performed stunts at county fairs and carnivals, often on the Wall of Death, to earn money. During this time, she made eight trips across America by herself. It wasn't safe for a girl to be traveling alone, much less a Black girl. Because of Jim Crow laws and racial prejudice, Bessie wasn't welcome in most motels or restaurants. Most people thought girls had no business riding motorcycles. But Bessie said, "I knew the Lord would take care of me and he did."

After a life of wandering, Bessie settled in Miami, Florida, in the 1950s. She founded the Iron Horse Motorcycle Club. She owned 27 Harley-Davidsons in her lifetime. Bessie died in 1993 in her early 80s. All her life, she fought against the stereotypes of what girls should do. She was not shy about telling the world, "I never was like anybody else." "If I don't ride, I won't live. And so, I never did quit."

In 2002, Bessie was inducted into the American Motorcycle Hall of Fame. Since 2013, hundreds of motorcycle riders have joined the Bessie Stringfield All Female Ride that goes from Georgia to Wisconsin. It is still uncommon to see women on motorcycles. The Motorcycle Industry Council did a survey in 2015. They found out that women motorcycle riders make up only 14% of the total motorcycle riding population in the U.S. In Bessie's day, women motorcycle riders were as rare as comets in the sky.